TALES OF EVA AND LUCAS

WRITTEN BY DELIA BERLIN

ILLUSTRATED BY HAILEY QUERCIA

CUENTOS DE EVA Y LUCAS

ESCRITO POR DELIA BERLIN

ILUSTRADO POR HAILEY QUERCIA

To Kayeleyn,
Witer best
wishes,
Delie Berlin
Enjoy,
Hailey
Quercia

ISBN: 1491097833

ISBN 13: 9781491097830

Library of Congress Control Number: 2013914149

CreateSpace Independent Publishing Platform

North Charleston, South Carolina

For Eva

D. B.

For Gramma Carol

H. Q.

Para Eva

D. B.

Para Gramma Carol

H. Q.

Chapters

The Magic Socks

The Three-Candy Problem

The Cutest Ugly Puppy

Capítulos

Las Medias Mágicas

El Problema de los Tres Caramelos

El Perrito Más Lindo y Más Feo

The Magic Socks

Las Medias Mágicas

Eva had a great imagination. Sometimes, like when she was painting, this was a good thing. But when she was trying to sleep, she would imagine monsters and get scared.

Eva tenía una gran imaginación. A veces, como cuando pintaba, eso era bueno... Pero cuando trataba de dormir, imaginaba monstruos y se asustaba.

One day, while Eva and her neighbor Lucas were playing together, she told him about her night fears. Lucas felt sorry for his friend… he had always felt magically protected in his sleep.

Un día, mientras Eva y su vecino Lucas jugaban, Eva le confió sus miedos nocturnos. Lucas se apenó por su amiga… él siempre se había sentido mágicamente protegido en su sueño.

Back home Lucas looked around his bedroom. He couldn't see anything magical. But as he got ready for bed he realized that his sleeping socks made him feel safe and relaxed.

The next day Lucas invited Eva to his house to get a special present. Eva hurried to Lucas' house, where he gave her his socks. *"Wear them when you go to bed and you won't be afraid of monsters…"* said Lucas.

De regreso en su casa Lucas estudió su dormitorio. No veía nada mágico. Pero cuando se preparaba para acostarse se dio cuenta de que sus medias de dormir lo hacían sentir seguro y relajado.

Al día siguiente Lucas invitó a Eva a su casa para darle un regalo especial. Eva se apresuró a ir a lo de Lucas, donde él le ofreció sus medias. "Si las usas para dormir no temerás a los monstruos…" explicó Lucas.

That night, Eva put on the sleeping socks and got ready for bed. She was tired and as soon as she placed her head on her pillow, she fell asleep.

The next morning, Eva realized that she hadn't been bothered by any thoughts of monsters. The magic socks had worked!

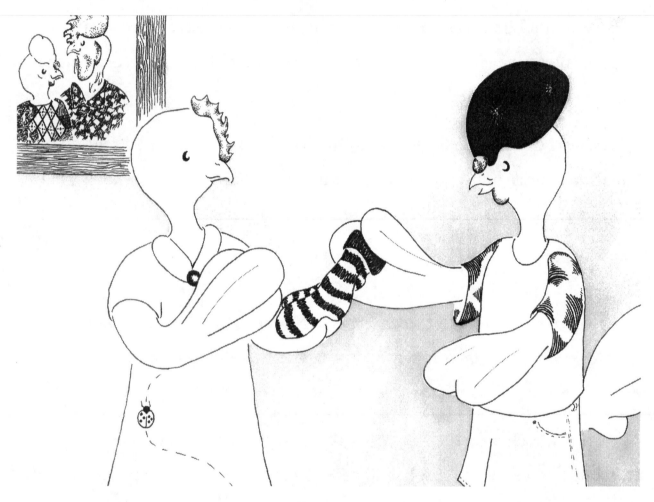

Esa noche, Eva se puso las medias de dormir y se preparó para acostarse. Estaba muy cansada y en cuanto apoyó su cabeza en la almohada se quedó dormida.

A la mañana siguiente Eva se dio cuenta de que no había imaginado monstruos. ¡Las medias mágicas habían funcionado!

Eva called Lucas to thank him. Lucas sounded very tired… Without his socks he had been awake all night in fear!

Eva llamó a Lucas para darle las gracias. Lucas sonaba muy cansado…
¡Sin sus medias no había podido dormir en toda la noche por miedos!

This was a problem. But now that Lucas had given his socks to his best friend, he couldn't ask for them back.

Eva liked her magic socks but felt bad for her friend. She used her great imagination to figure out a solution. If the sleeping socks were really magical, one should work as well as two.

That night, Eva got in her bed with one sock on her right foot. At Lucas' home, he went to sleep with one sock on his left foot. And both friends slept in peace through the night!

Esto era un problema. Pero ahora que Lucas le había regalado sus medias a su mejor amiga, no podía pedírselas de vuelta.

A Eva le gustaban sus medias mágicas pero se sentía mal por su amigo. Usó su gran imaginación para descubrir una solución. Si las medias eran realmente mágicas, una tendría que funcionar tan bien como dos.

Esa noche, Eva se acostó con una media en su pie derecho. En su casa, Lucas se acostó con una media en su pie izquierdo. ¡Y los dos amigos durmieron en paz toda la noche!

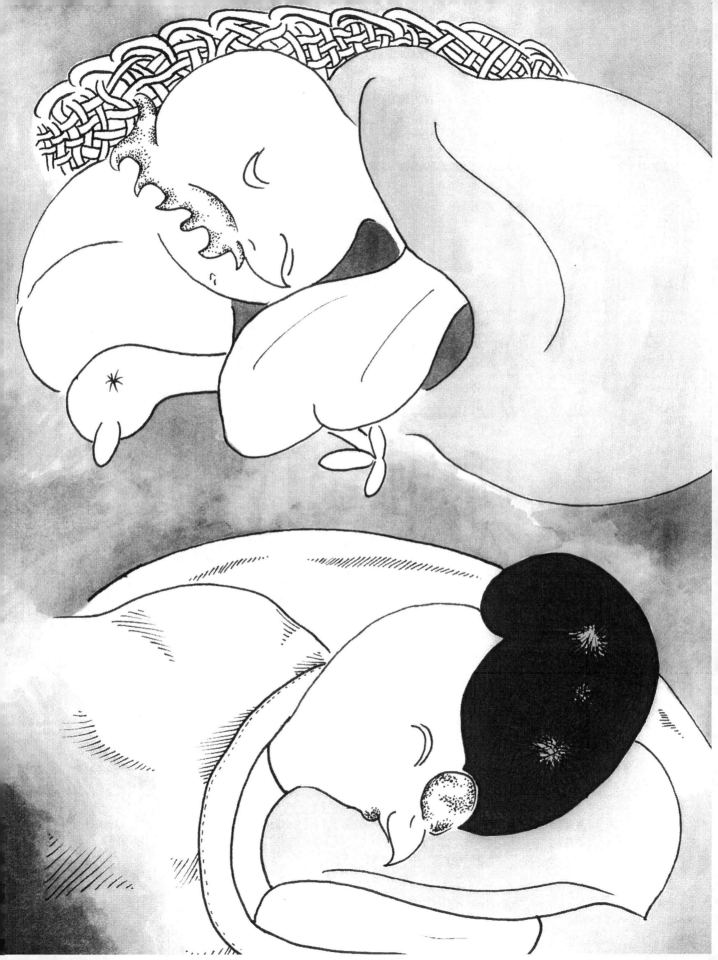

Later that day Eva and Lucas went to play at the park. Both of them were still wearing one sleeping sock each. They laughed as they each stuck a foot out and said "*The two of us really make a good pair!*"

Esa tarde los amigos fueron a jugar al parque. Ambos todavía tenían puestos una media cada uno. Rieron al extender sus pies, exclamando: "¡Entre nosotros, formamos un buen par!"

The Three-Candy Problem

El Problema de los Tres Caramelos

Eva and Lucas were good friends. They enjoyed playing and sharing things perfectly fairly.

Eva y Lucas eran buenos amigos. Disfrutaban jugar y compartir todo de manera perfectamente justa.

Each time they walked to the playground, they stopped by the vending machine at the corner store. They each put one coin in the machine and got a bag of hard candy to share.

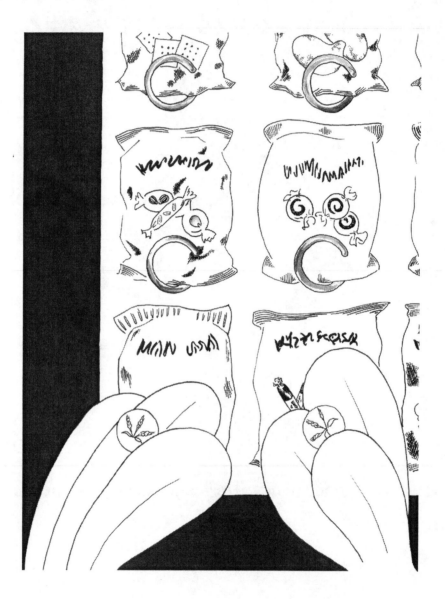

Cada vez que iban al parque, paraban en el negocio de la esquina para comprar caramelos en la máquina de golosinas. Cada uno ponía una moneda en la máquina y sacaban una bolsa de caramelos para compartir.

At the playground, Eva and Lucas opened their bag of candy under the shade of a big tree. There were usually four pieces: two for Eva and two for Lucas, and that was perfectly fair.

One day, as Eva and Lucas sat down to share their candy they discovered that the bag only had three pieces. And no matter how hard they tried, they could not divide them fairly.

En el parque, Eva y Lucas abrían la bolsa de caramelos a la sombra de un gran árbol. Usualmente había cuatro caramelos: dos para Eva y dos para Lucas, y eso era perfectamente justo.

Un día, cuando Eva y Lucas se sentaron a compartir sus caramelos, descubrieron que la bolsa tenía sólo tres. Y aunque trataban y trataban de dividirlos justamente, no podían.

If Eva took two pieces, there was only one left for Lucas. If Lucas took two pieces, there was only one left for Eva…

Just as Eva and Lucas were puzzling over this, their neighbor Max walked by. Eva and Lucas explained their problem to Max.

Si Eva tomaba dos caramelos, quedaba sólo uno para Lucas. Si Lucas tomaba dos caramelos, quedaba sólo uno para Eva…

Mientras Eva y Lucas trataban de resolver esto, su vecino Max pasó por allí. Eva y Lucas le explicaron el problema a Max.

Max was delighted to help. He decided that Eva and Lucas take one piece of candy each, while he took the third one as a favor. Before Eva and Lucas could react, Max was skipping past them and enjoying his free candy.

Lucas was happy to have settled the matter so he could at least eat his share. But Eva couldn't stop thinking about Max eating **their** piece of candy.

A few days later, Eva and Lucas once again walked to the playground. They stopped by the vending machine and got a bag of candy. They sat under the tree and opened the bag, hoping that it would have four pieces, but once again it had only three.

Max se alegró de poder ayudar. Decidió que Eva y Lucas comieran un caramelo cada uno, mientras él les hacía el favor de comerse el tercero. Antes de que Eva y Lucas pudieran reaccionar, Max se fue a los saltos comiendo su caramelo.

Lucas se alegró de haber resuelto la situación para comerse su caramelo. Pero Eva no podía dejar de pensar en Max comiéndose su tercer caramelo.

Unos días después, Eva y Lucas volvieron al parque. Pasaron por la máquina de golosinas y sacaron una bolsa de caramelos. Se sentaron bajo el árbol y abrieron la bolsa esperando que tuviera cuatro caramelos, pero una vez más tenía sólo tres.

Lucas suggested calling on Max again. But Eva had a different idea. *"Lucas, please take two pieces. I will be happy with one..."* said Eva.

On their walk home, Lucas was quiet. *"Are you OK?"* asked Eva. *"Next time we get three pieces of candy, I would like **you** to have two..."* said Lucas, and so continued this pair, always being perfectly fair.

Lucas sugirió llamar nuevamente a Max. Pero Eva tenía otra idea. "Lucas, por favor toma dos. A mí me basta con uno..." dijo Eva.

De regreso a casa, Lucas estaba muy callado. Eva le preguntó si todo estaba bien. "La próxima vez que tengamos tres caramelos, quisiera que tú tomes dos..." dijo Lucas, y así continúo este par, siendo siempre perfectamente justo.

The Cutest Ugly Puppy

El Perrito Más Lindo y Más Feo

When Eva heard that Mrs. Otero's dog had seven puppies, she asked Lucas to go see them with her. The friends walked together briskly, eager to see the pups.

Cuando Eva se enteró de que la perra de la Sra. Otero había tenido siete cachorritos, le pidió a Lucas que la acompañara a verlos. Los amigos caminaban con prisa, ansiosos de ver a los perritos.

Mrs. Otero was playing with the puppies in her yard. She encouraged Eva and Lucas to pet them. The puppies were soft and gentle. They were small, and spotted brown, black and white.

La Sra. Otero estaba jugando con los cachorros en su jardín. Insistió en que Eva y Lucas los acariciaran. Los perritos eran dóciles y suaves. Eran pequeños, con manchas marrones, negras y blancas.

Eva thought that one puppy was by far the cutest, and she asked Mrs. Otero if they were all available for adoption. A few were spoken for, but most were still free to good homes.

Lucas also liked the puppies and thought they were very cute. All except one that to him looked very strange and quite ugly.

Eva's birthday was coming up and she asked for a puppy as her present. Her mom liked the idea of getting a family pet instead of a store puppy.

Eva pensaba que uno de los perritos era definitivamente el más lindo, y le preguntó a la Sra. Otero si todos los cachorros se podían adoptar. Algunos ya estaban prometidos, pero los demás estaban disponibles gratis para buenas familias.

A Lucas también le gustaban los perritos y pensaba que eran muy lindos. Todos excepto uno que le parecía muy raro y bastante feo.

El cumpleaños de Eva se acercaba y ella pidió un perrito de regalo. A su madre le agradó la idea de adoptar un perrito de familia en vez de comprar uno.

Eva called Mrs. Otero to reserve a puppy for the end of the week. Then she prepared a sleeping basket, bowls for food and water, and started reading about dog training.

Eva llamó a la Sra. Otero para reservar un cachorro para el fin de semana. Luego preparó una canasta de dormir, fuentes para comida y agua, y comenzó a leer sobre entrenamiento de perritos.

The day that Eva was going to pick up her puppy, she woke up with a fever and her mother made her stay home. Eva couldn't wait to have her puppy, so she asked Lucas to pick it up for her.

Lucas' mother didn't want him to get sick also, so she asked him to deliver the puppy to Eva's parents without staying to play with Eva. Lucas agreed and headed to Mrs. Otero's.

Mrs. Otero told Lucas that she had reserved the last puppy for Eva. When she handed it to him, Lucas was shocked to see that it was the ugly puppy!

El día que Eva iba a buscar su cachorrito, se despertó con fiebre y su madre la hizo quedar en casa. Eva no quería seguir esperando, entonces le pidió a Lucas que fuera a buscar su perrito.

La madre de Lucas no quería que él se contagiara, entonces le pidió a Lucas que dejara el cachorro con los padres de Eva sin quedarse a jugar con ella. Lucas aceptó y se dirigió a lo de la Sra. Otero.

La Sra. Otero le dijo a Lucas que había reservado el último cachorrito para Eva. ¡Y cuando se lo entregó, Lucas notó alarmado que era el cachorro feo!

Lucas tried to smile, thanked Mrs. Otero and left with the puppy. Eva had a good heart and she would surely love any puppy. Wouldn't she?

Lucas worried about disappointing his friend. The puppy was cuddly but weird looking, with a pink nose and droopy ears. Now Lucas was relieved that he couldn't stay to see Eva.

Eva's mother seemed pleased and thanked Lucas. He left in a hurry, afraid that Eva might come out while he was still there.

Lucas trató de sonreír, le dio las gracias a la Sra. Otero y se fue con el perrito. Eva tenía buen corazón y seguramente iba a querer a cualquier cachorrito. ¿O no?

Lucas temía desilusionar a su amiga. El perrito era mimoso pero raro, con la nariz rosada y las orejas caídas… Ahora Lucas se sentía aliviado de no poder quedarse a ver a Eva.

La madre de Eva parecía contenta y agradeció a Lucas. Lucas se apresuró a irse, temeroso de que Eva apareciera mientras él todavía estaba allí.

When Lucas got home, his mom told him that Eva had called and wanted him to call her back right away. Now Lucas would have to explain that the puppy was the only one left… Maybe Mrs. Otero would take it back…

Cuando Lucas llegó a su casa, su madre le dijo que Eva había llamado y quería que Lucas la llamara enseguida. Ahora Lucas tendría que explicarle que el cachorro era el único que quedaba. Quizá la Sra. Otero lo aceptaría de vuelta…

Lucas's heart was racing as Eva's phone rang. Suddenly, he heard her voice sounding happy and excited. Eva was delighted because he had brought her the *cutest* puppy. It was just the one she had liked best!

El corazón de Lucas daba saltos mientras el teléfono de Eva sonaba... De repente, escuchó la voz de Eva, feliz y excitada. Eva estaba encantada porque le había traído el perrito más lindo. ¡Era su cachorro favorito!

Delia Berlin and Hailey Quercia

Delia Berlin was born and raised in Argentina but has spent most of her life in Connecticut. Her professional career has focused on education and administration. With graduate degrees in both Physics and Family Studies, she also worked in early intervention and taught child development at the college level. With her children's writing Delia seeks to spark new insights and to convey joy through age-appropriate humor, while expanding vocabulary and social skills. She is also the author of *Training Captive Bred Parrots* and *Mature Bird Care*.

Hailey Quercia is a biology student with a lifelong interest in art. She is a member of the *Connecticut Women Artists* and studies art privately. She works in graphite, watercolor, pen and ink, colored pencil and pastel. Many of her works feature animals as subjects. Hailey especially enjoys drawing and painting birds. In addition to group and solo art shows, her work has been shown in several juried art exhibits and she has won both local and state awards.

Delia Berlin nació y creció en Argentina pero ha pasado la mayor parte de su vida en Connecticut. Su carrera profesional se ha enfocado en educación y administración. Con títulos avanzados en Física y Estudios de Familia, también ha trabajado en intervención infantil y ha enseñado desarrollo de niños a nivel terciario. Con sus cuentos para niños Delia espera provocar descubrimientos y transmitir alegría a través de humor apropiado para sus edades, y al mismo tiempo expandir vocabulario y destrezas sociales. También es autora de Training Captive Bred Parrots y Mature Bird Care.

Hailey Quercia es una estudiante de biología con constante interés en arte. Pertenece a la sociedad de Connecticut Women Artists y estudia arte privadamente. Trabaja en grafito, acuarela, tinta y pluma, lápiz de color y pastel. Muchas de sus obras representan animales. A Hailey le apasiona dibujar y pintar pájaros. Además de exhibiciones individuales y de grupo, ha participado en varios concursos con jurado y ha recibido premios a nivel local y estatal.

CPSIA information can be obtained at www.ICGtesting.com
Printed in the USA
BVOW06s1909040314

346654BV00002B/6/P

"The wonderful books in the Weird series are great resources to help build young children's social skills to address and prevent bullying."

—**Trudy Ludwig,** children's advocate and best-selling author of *Confessions of a Former Bully*

"I love this series. Kids are sure to empathize with the characters and recognize their own power to stop bullying."

—**Dr. Michele Borba,** internationally recognized child expert and author of *The Big Book of Parenting Solutions*

"The well-drawn characters have real problems with . . . credible resolutions. This [series] should find a home in every school library."

—*Kirkus*

"The books stand alone as separate titles, but they're much more effective when utilized together to give a complete view of how the main characters are feeling and the outside events that help shape their roles."

—*School Library Journal*

"An excellent tool for teaching school-age children good mental health techniques to survive and grow beyond bullying."

—*Children's Bookwatch*, **Reviewer's Choice**

"A good discussion starter."

—*Booklist*

"Incredibly insightful . . . a must-own for educators."

—*Imagination Soup*

WEIRD!

A Story About Dealing with Bullying in Schools

by Erin Frankel

illustrated by Paula Heaphy

free spirit
PUBLISHING®

Acknowledgments

Heartfelt thanks to Judy Galbraith, Meg Bratsch, Steven Hauge, Michelle Lee Lagerroos, and Margie Lisovskis at Free Spirit for their expertise, support, and dedication to making the world a better place for children. Special gratitude to Kelsey, Sofia, and Gabriela for their enthusiasm and ideas during the creation of this book. Appreciation to Naomi Drew for her helpful comments. Thanks also to Alvaro, Thomas, Ann, Paul, Ros, Beth, and all our family and friends for their creative insight and encouragement.

Library of Congress Cataloging-in-Publication Data
Frankel, Erin.
  Weird! / by Erin Frankel ; illustrated by Paula Heaphy.
    p. cm. — (Weird series ; bk. 1)
  ISBN 978-1-57542-398-2 (Hardcover)
  1. Bullying—Juvenile literature. 2. Bullying in schools—Juvenile literature. 3. Individual differences in children—Juvenile literature.
  4. Self-confidence in children—Juvenile literature. I. Heaphy, Paula. II. Title.
  BF637.B85F73 2012
  302.34'3—dc23

                                                                                      2012006157

ISBN: 978-1-57542-437-8

Reading Level Grade 2; Interest Level Ages 5–9;
Fountas & Pinnell Guided Reading Level M

Edited by Meg Bratsch
Cover and interior design by Michelle Lee Lagerroos
Photo of Erin Frankel by Gabriela Cadahia; photo of Paula Heaphy by Travis Huggett

10 9 8 7
Printed in Hong Kong
P17200219

Free Spirit Publishing Inc.
6325 Sandburg Road, Suite 100
Minneapolis, MN 55427-3674
(612) 338-2068
help4kids@freespirit.com
www.freespirit.com

Free Spirit offers competitive pricing.
Contact edsales@freespirit.com for pricing information on multiple quantity purchases.

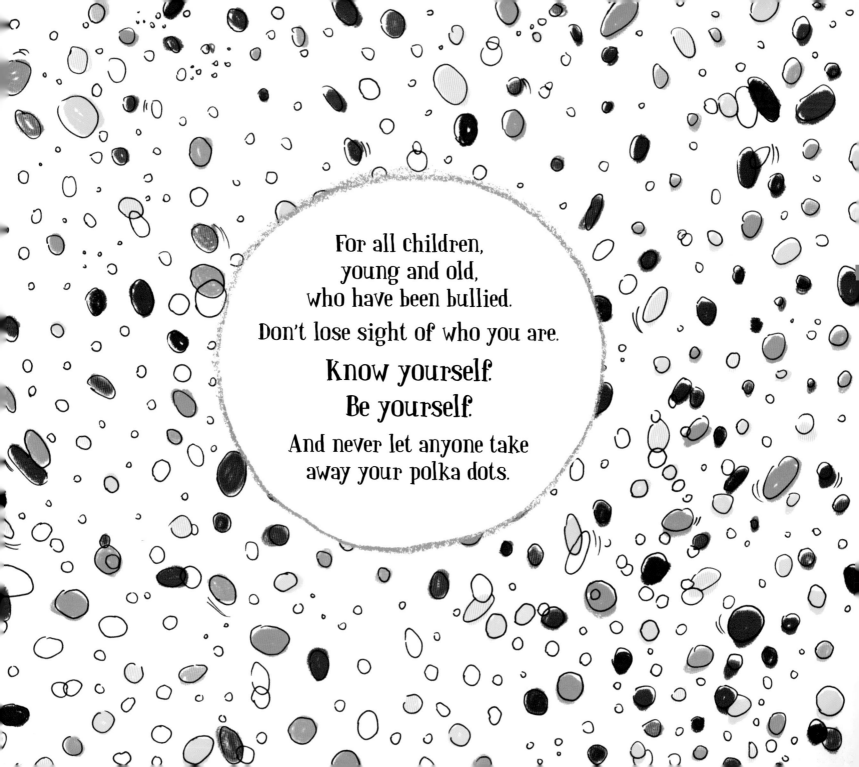

For all children,
young and old,
who have been bullied.

Don't lose sight of who you are.

Know yourself.

Be yourself.

And never let anyone take
away your polka dots.

Hi. My name is Luisa and I have a problem.

There is a girl in my class named Sam who thinks that everything I do is

WEIRD!

I raise my hand to answer a question in math,
and she says I'm WEIRD.

I try telling a **funny** joke
at lunch, and **she** says I'm . . .

WEIRD!

Guess I'll just
be quiet.

LUISA

I give my **mom** a kiss when she picks me up from school, and Sam says I'm . . .

WEIRD!

Maybe Mom can wait
for me in the car.

I say something in **Spanish** to my **dad**, and she says
I'm WEIRD.

"Hi, Dad."

Guess it's "**Hi, Dad**" from now on.

"Weird!"

I wear my **favorite** polka dot boots,
and she says I'm WEIRD.

It's strange.
I keep changing what I do,
but she doesn't change at all.

She still says
I'm WEIRD.

It seems like weird is the only word
she knows, and I don't know any words.

13

"Where did all your polka dots go, Luisa?"

I don't even feel like **myself** anymore.

14

Everyone else **misses** the way I **used to be**.
Everyone else, including **me**.

Who should I talk to?

What will I say?

What did I do to deserve this?

I wish it all
would just
go away.

"I found your boots."

After talking to Mom, I've been **thinking**. Maybe it's time for **one more**

change.

19

So I put my **favorite** polka dot **boots** back on. Only this time, before **Sam** could say anything,

I said, "Boy, it feels **great** to be back in **these** again!"

21

I told another **funny** joke at lunch and **laughed** along with my friends. When she said **WEIRD**, I kept on laughing.

I didn't hide my feelings
when I got the **right** answer in math.

I told my dad I loved him in **Spanish**.

"¡Te quiero muchííísimo, Papa!"

"I missed you today, Mom!"

I let my **mom** know how **happy I was** to see her when she picked me up from school.

24

25

I discovered something **really** **amazing!**

The more I **act** like
I don't care what **she** says,
the more **I really don't care.**

And the more she **thinks**
I don't care,
the more she **leaves me alone.**

Now **that's** really . . .

27

28

RD!

29

I guess I'll just be **me** from now on!

30

Luisa's Notes

Boy, am I glad I got my polka dots back—and they're not *weird* at all! Here are some things I can remember so I won't lose them again:

When I feel nervous, scared, or sad, I can think positive thoughts.

Everyone has the right to feel safe and respected, including me.

I am not to blame when someone chooses to bully me.

Remember there are people who care and want to help me if I ask them to.

Don't give anyone the power to take away what makes me special.

Sam's Notes

It used to bother Luisa when I called her "weird," but now she looks happy and confident . . . which makes me feel not so *tough* anymore. Here are some things I've been thinking about:

Trying to bully someone who ignores me isn't any fun.

Owning up to my behavior is going to be hard, but maybe it's worth it.

Until Luisa acted confident, I felt like I had power over her.

Guess bullying won't get me what I want after all.

Hearing others stand up for Luisa made me step back and think about what I was doing.

Jayla's Notes

I'm so glad Luisa is back to being herself. Now I know that I can *dare* to stand up for someone who is being bullied. Here are some other things I've learned as a bystander to bullying:

Doing what's right can be hard at first, but it always feels good in the long run.

Asking others for help makes a big difference.

Real friendship is about standing up for each other.

Encouraging Luisa to be confident in herself helped Sam stop bullying her.

Join Luisa's Confidence Club!

Acting confident isn't always easy. But the more you practice, the better you'll get. I found out that I can make some really simple changes to look, sound, and feel more confident. I can . . .

Stand up tall with my shoulders back and my head held high.

Look others in the eye—*not* down at the floor.

Speak clearly so people can understand me.

Smile and laugh if I want to!

Turn and walk away calmly when I don't like what is happening.

Tell an adult if I or someone else needs help.*

Confident means believing in yourself and your abilities.

*Telling vs. Tattling

Nobody wants to be a tattletale. But tattling on a person for something small (like picking her nose!) is very *different* from telling an adult when someone needs help. If you were being bullied, you'd want someone to help you, right?

While I am doing all this on the *outside*, I am also making changes on the *inside*. Instead of thinking negative thoughts that make me feel nervous inside, I think positive thoughts that make me feel calm and confident. Here's what I think inside my head when Sam is around:

> "I am going to walk by and choose not to listen to what she is saying."

> "I am *not* going to let her ruin my day."

> "I am calm and confident."

> "I don't have to worry about what she thinks."

> "Many people like me just the way I am."

> "I can always ask for help if I need it."

Can you think of other ways to look and feel confident? Share them with your friends and classmates!

Confidence Club: Recycle Your Thoughts

Help me recycle my negative thoughts into positive ones. It's easier than you think!

1. Cut out eight circles from a sheet of paper. These are your polka dots.

2. Find four of my negative thoughts in the book and write them on four of the polka dots.

3. For each negative thought, think of a positive thought to write on the other four polka dots. Then, color and decorate the *positive* polka dots.

4. Now, crinkle up the negative polka dots and toss them in the recycling bin.

5. Let's put my recycled thoughts to good use! Decorate your room with the positive polka dots. Make a mobile or a card for someone.

Next, try recycling your *own* negative thoughts into positive thoughts. With a little practice, you'll be thinking positively in no time!

Confidence Club: Step in the Right Direction

At first, I was nervous about putting my polka dot boots back on. I wondered what Sam would say when I walked by her. But when I focused on walking *away* from Sam and *toward* people who care about me, it wasn't as hard to step in the right direction!

You never know when someone might need *your* help to step in the right direction. Why not make your own poster to show you care?

1. Write "Step in the Right Direction" at the top of a poster board.

2. Trace each of your feet twice on the poster board. Draw a picture of yourself next to the last footprint.

3. Write, draw, or paste caring messages inside your footprints. You can use some of the caring messages I got in this book if you'd like.

4. Give the poster to a friend to show her or him how to step *away* from someone who is being mean and *toward* someone who cares—you!

Can you think of more fun activities we can do in our Confidence Club? Share them with your classmates and friends.

"I miss your funny jokes."

"You are wonderful just the way you are."

"Love those polka dots!"

"It's not your fault."

A Note to Parents, Teachers, and Other Caring Adults

Every day, millions of children are subjected to bullying in the form of name-calling, threats, insults, belittling, taunting, rumors, and racist slurs—and still more are witnesses to it. Verbal bullying, which can begin as early as preschool, accounts for 70 percent of reported bullying and is often a stepping stone to other types of aggression, including physical, relational, and online bullying. Hurtful words, both spoken and written, chip away at a child's budding sense of self, leaving fear, shame, and self-doubt in its place. As caring adults, how can we help children feel safe, respected, and confident in who they are?

We can start by holding children who bully others accountable for their behavior, while modeling and encouraging positive choices. We can help bystanders explore safe and effective ways to stand up for those who are being bullied. And through books such as *Weird!*, we can help kids like Luisa, who are targets of bullying, understand how to ask for help and how the words they say to themselves—their "self-talk"—can counteract hurtful words from others. Simple changes in the way kids think and act can have a positive impact on their self-confidence and influence bullying outcomes.

Reflection Questions for *Weird!*

The story told in *Weird!* illustrates a fictional situation, but it is one that many kids will likely relate to even if their experiences have been different. Following are some questions and activities to encourage reflection and dialogue as you read *Weird!* Referring to the main characters by name will help children make connections: *Luisa* is the target of the bullying, *Jayla* is a bystander to the bullying, and *Sam* initiates the bullying.

Important: **Online bullying (called *cyberbullying*) is a real threat among elementary-age children, given the increased use of smartphones and computers in school and at home. It's also the most difficult type of bullying to stop, because it's less apparent to onlookers. Be sure to include cyberbullying in all of your discussions about bullying with kids.**

Page 1: How do you think Luisa is feeling? Why do you think she feels that way?

Pages 2–11: What does Luisa do after Sam (the girl in her class) calls her "weird"? Why do you think she does that? Who are the other characters in the story? What are they doing as Sam bullies Luisa? What would you do if you saw someone being treated that way?

Pages 12–13: Luisa says, "It seems like *weird* is the only word she knows, and I don't know any words." What do you think she means?

Pages 14–15: Does Luisa look different on page 14? Why? Who are the characters on these two pages and why are they important?

Pages 16–17: Is it hard for Luisa to ask for help? Why? Who can you go to for help if you are being bullied? (**Note:** *Many kids suffer in silence when they are bullied, because they don't know who to ask for help or what to say. They might even think they deserve the bullying, worry that others won't believe them, assume they will get in trouble, or fear retaliation by the person doing the bullying. Assure kids that, while it may be difficult, it's important to ask for help—and to ask as many times as it takes to end the bullying.*)

Pages 18–19: What is Jayla (the girl in the background) doing with Luisa's boots on page 18? Why? What is Luisa doing with all the negative thoughts she wrote down before, and why?

> *Note:* **The activity on page 36 tells kids how to recycle negative thoughts into positive thoughts. This can be a complex process, so be sure to guide them through the steps.**

Pages 20–21: What are the other characters in the hallway doing and saying? How do you think that makes Luisa feel? How do you think that makes Sam feel?

Pages 22–25: What is different about Luisa on these pages? What is different about Sam? Why do you think Sam bullies? Why might other kids bully? Why is it wrong to bully?

Pages 26–31: What does Luisa discover? What are some things you can do to feel and look more confident? Let's rehearse them!

Overall: Which character in *Weird!* is most like you and why? What would you like to say to this character?

The Weird Series

The Weird series gives readers the opportunity to explore three very different perspectives on bullying: that of a child who is a target of bullying in *Weird!*, that of a bystander to bullying in *Dare!*, and that of a child who initiates bullying in *Tough!* Each book can be used alone or together with the other books in the series to build awareness and engage children in discussions related to bullying and encourage bullying prevention. If you are using the books as a series, consider doing the following activities with young readers.

Series Activity: Everyone Has a Role to Play

Discuss with children how we all have a role to play when it comes to ending bullying. Consider how it was easier for Luisa to start being herself again with the support from her family, her teachers, her classmates, and her friends. In small groups or as a class, role-play Luisa's story.

Series Activity: Memorable Moments

Have children fold a sheet of paper into three equal parts and label each part with one of the three book titles: *Weird!*, *Dare!*, and *Tough!* Invite children to draw what they think was the most important moment from each book in the corresponding section of the paper. Have children share their drawings and explain why they were memorable moments.

Series Activity: Circle of Courage

Ask children to consider specific acts of courage by others that made a difference for Luisa, Jayla, and Sam. Mount a large paper circle onto a bulletin board and write "Circle of Courage" in the center. Place a container with colorful paper polka dots, stars, and hearts next to the circle. Encourage children to add shapes to the circle whenever they witness an act of courage that helps prevent or stop bullying.

Series Activity: What Comes Next?

Weird! Dare! Tough! . . . what comes next? Ask children to imagine and make predictions about what happens to the characters in the next book. Encourage them to consider the main characters: *Luisa, Jayla,* and *Sam,* as well as the peripheral characters in the books: *Emily, Thomas, Patrick, Will, Mr. C.,* and *Alex.* Then have kids create and present their own book title and storyboard.

About the Author and Illustrator

Erin Frankel has a master's degree in English education and is passionate about parenting, teaching, and writing. She taught ESL in Madrid, Spain, before moving to Pittsburgh, Pennsylvania, with her husband Alvaro and their three daughters, Gabriela, Sofia, and Kelsey. Erin knows firsthand what it feels like to be bullied, and she hopes her stories will help children stay true to who they are and help put an end to bullying. She and her longtime friend and illustrator Paula Heaphy believe in the power of kindness and are grateful to be able to spread that message through their work. In her free time, you'll find Erin hiking in the woods with her family and doggie, Bella, or getting some words down on paper wherever and whenever she can.

Paula Heaphy is a print and pattern designer in the fashion industry. She's an explorer of all artistic mediums from glassblowing to shoemaking, but her biggest love is drawing. She jumped at the chance to illustrate her friend Erin's story, having been bullied herself as a child. As the character of Luisa came to life on paper, Paula felt her path in life suddenly shift into focus. She lives in Brooklyn, New York, where she hopes to use her creativity to light up the hearts of children for years to come.

The Weird Series

by Erin Frankel, illustrated by Paula Heaphy. 48 pp. Ages 5–9.

More Bully Free Kids® Books from Free Spirit

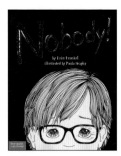

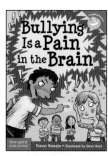

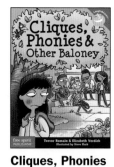

Nobody!
*by Erin Frankel,
illustrated by Paula Heaphy*
48 pp. Ages 5–9.

Stand Up to Bullying!
*by Phyllis Kaufman Goodstein
and Elizabeth Verdick,
illustrated by Steve Mark*
128 pp. Ages 8–13.

**Bullying Is a Pain
in the Brain**
*by Trevor Romain,
illustrated by Steve Mark*
112 pp. Ages 8–13.

**Cliques, Phonies
& Other Baloney**
*by Trevor Romain and Elizabeth Verdick,
illustrated by Steve Mark*
112 pp. Ages 8–13.

For pricing information, to place an order, or to request a free catalog, contact:

free spirit PUBLISHING®

6325 Sandburg Road • Suite 100 • Minneapolis, MN 55427-3674 • toll-free 800.735.7323 • local 612.338.2068
fax 612.337.5050 • help4kids@freespirit.com • www.freespirit.com